Monster Eyeballs

Titles in the Bunch:

Baby Bear Comes Home

Big Dog and Little Dog Visit the Moon

Clumsy Clumps and the Baby Moon

Delilah Digs for Treasure

Dilly and the Goody-Goody · Happy Sad

Horse in the House · I don't want to say Yes!

Juggling with Jeremy · Keeping Secrets

Mabel and Max · Magnificent Mummies

Midnight in Memphis · Millie's Party

Monster Eyeballs · Mouse Flute · The Nut Map

Owl in the House · Peg · Promise you won't be cross

· Riff-Raff Rabbit · Rosie and the Robbers

· Runaway Fred · Tom's Hats

First published in Great Britain 1999 by Mammoth
an imprint of Egmont Children's Books Limited
239 Kensington High Street, London W8 6SA
Published in hardback by Heinemann Library,
a division of Reed Educational and Professional Publishing Limited
by arrangement with Egmont Children's Books Limited.
Text copyright © Jacqueline Wilson 1999
Illustrations © Stephen Lewis 1999
The Author and Illustrator have asserted their moral rights.
Paperback ISBN 0 7497 2814 0
Hardback ISBN 0 434 97640 7
10 9 8 7 6 5 4 3 2 1
A CIP catalogue record for this title is available from the British Library.
Printed and bound in Dubai by Oriental Press Limited.

Jacqueline Wilson

Monster Eyeballs

Illustrated by Stephen Lewis

Blue Bananas

For

Thorne and Franca

J.W.

For

my mother

S.L.

Kate liked going to school.

Kate liked Art. She liked painting a picture of a lady in a long red dress.

She liked painting her nails red too.

Kate liked Story Time. One day the teacher read them *The Gingerbread Man*. Then she gave everyone a gingerbread man to eat.

Kate liked her best friend Amy most of all.

There were a few bad things about school. Kate didn't like the toilets.

Kate didn't like being told off by her teacher.

Most of all, Kate didn't like Mark. He was the biggest boy in the class. He was horrible.

It was a good job Kate

had a best friend.

But one day Amy didn't come to school.

She had chickenpox and

stayed at home.

Kate didn't feel happy without Amy.

Mark kept pestering her.

Mark couldn't do anything too terrible in the classroom – but at playtime Kate knew she was in for trouble. Big trouble!

Mark took Kate's chocolate at playtime.

Kate didn't have Amy to comfort her.

Kate missed Amy very much.

Amy wasn't back at school the next day
– or the next – or the next. Kate didn't
want to go to school without Amy.

I'm going to have chickenpox too.

Kate couldn't fool her mum. Mum knew

Kate was missing Amy.

Mum gave Kate a special strawberry

chocolate bar to eat at playtime.

Kate hid the chocolate in her pocket. But Kate couldn't fool Mark. 'I'm hungry,' he said. 'Give me some chocolate.'

Kate wanted to tell the teacher but she
was too scared.

You tell and I'll twist your doll's head off.

Kate told her big brother

Robbie instead.

Robbie told Mark he'd twist *his* head off.

Mark told his big brother Andrew.

Robbie and Andrew had a big fight.

Robbie and Andrew had to stay in after

school. But they didn't fight any more.

They made friends.

Kate and Mark were amazed.

Mark was extra annoying in the classroom . . .

. . . Mark was extra annoying in the playground too.

Kate phoned her best friend
Amy to tell her.

I miss you, Amy.

'I'm all spotty and itchy,' said Amy. 'Mum's
painted the spots with pink stuff and she's
painted my nails pink to match.'

Kate was pleased when it was Saturday.

She didn't have to go to school.

Robbie was pleased too.

It was his birthday.

Robbie was having a party. He had invited three friends. Kate was invited too. She wore her special party frock and felt ever so grown up.

Robbie wore his new football strip. His friends wore football strips too. One of his friends was Andrew. Guess who Andrew brought with him!

Robbie opened his presents. He got very
excited.

Everyone got very excited.

Mum told them to go out in the garden and play football. Everyone liked that idea.

Kate wanted to play football too.

Kate was good at football. She scored three goals.

Kate forgot she was wearing

her party frock.

Mum had made a very good birthday tea. Robbie had a special football birthday cake.

After tea Mum put

on a cartoon.

Then she went to do the washing up and

Robbie put on a different video. It was a

very scary video about monsters.

Kate had seen it before.

She knew when to shut her eyes.

Mum got cross when she saw what they were watching. She switched the television off and told them to play party games. They played Squeak, Piggy, Squeak.

Kate was the Piggy

They played murder in the dark.

Kate got murdered.

Then they played the Feely Game.

Everyone took turns to go into the kitchen,

blindfolded. 'Feel the monster eyeballs,

Kate,' said Robbie.

But Kate had played
this game before. She
knew they weren't really
monster eyeballs.

Can't fool
me. They're grapes
not eyeballs.

Mark was the last to have a turn. He had
never played the Feely Game before.

Mark burst into tears. He had to have a
cuddle with Kate's mum. Kate felt a bit
sorry for him.

Mark didn't bother Kate at school after that birthday party. He wished he hadn't been so nasty to her before. He wanted to be her friend now!

Then Amy got better at last. Kate liked going to school again. 'Mark's O.K. now,' she said to Amy, 'but if he pesters us again I know just what to do.'